AT APPROXIMATELY 9:00p.m. on February 17th, 2012, seven-month old Cameron Harris was drowned by his mother in a mobile home kitchen sink. Once expired, the mother, Fern (Travettie) Harris, handed her son to her husband, Brian, who proceeded to leave Tamarac Village in his rusted blue 1994 Chevrolet S10. Brian disposed of the body by placing Cameron on a sheet of ice stretching from ditch wall to ditch wall just off of Pere Marquette Road. The police report, as written by the first responder, Mason County Sherriff's Department Deputy Alan Kramer, stated that a sky-blue blanket had been wrapped around Cameron's body, covering all but his head.

Baby Cameron, as he'd become known in the media, was found just after 1:00a.m. on February 18th, 2012 by Zack Strauss. Strauss, a seventeen-year old senior at Ludington High School, said in an interview with the West Central Gazette minutes after fishtailing off Pere Marquette

Road and into the ditch where Baby Cameron lay: "I'd just dropped off my girlfriend, I hit a patch of ice, and-and-and I could've crushed him. Could've just smashed him." Emily Unting, our feature writer at the time, wrote that Zack then clapped once, lightly. "Just like that."

Brian's younger brother, James, scrawny and gap-toothed, stammered in disbelief during his interview with Channel 6, a bit spliced between shots of MCSD officers taking a compliant Brian and Fern into custody: "My brother's the only father I've ever had. He isn't capable of this. No way." He was the only one to cry on camera.

"They deserve to be tied up, those deranged toes inches from the flame," The Silver Fox, a 103.1FM (Petoskey, Michigan) radio personality known for the uncensored music he slipped in during early morning hours stated days after. "Maybe then they'd know the pain they have caused us all." The apology he was forced to make the following night wasn't issued with nearly as much conviction.

Fern's cousin, Lois (Travettie) Henslow, a receptionist for the Hindman/Crown marketing agency in Kalamazoo, placed frustrated hands on narrow hips and said little to Channel 3's cameras before getting into a dented Chevrolet Trailblazer parked blocks from the office: "She said she needed to talk. I should've listened. But, I ignored her. And now we're here."

Roger Burton, then mayor-elect of Ludington and father of a daughter killed by a drunk driver two years prior, with several microphones inches from his mouth, said to me, to all of us at the news conference outside of Mason County's Courthouse: "Brian and Fern Harris encompass all that is wrong with this world and have brought their evil upon our lovely and safe community. We eagerly await the results of their trial."

For four months the people not just of Ludington, but those across Michigan shouted to one another about Baby Cameron. And what the echos made clear was that they wanted—what the voices truly wanted—was closure through condemnation. They needed someone to blame, and in turn had reacted as if Baby Cameron—a Ludington trailer baby the majority, had it not been for his death, would never know of, or care for—had been deemed the state's child. A part of each citizen had seemingly died along with him.

I didn't share those feelings. I refused to believe that any part of me had died, that a part of me could. Which left me to struggle as I wrote column after column on Baby Cameron, as I worked to wrap my head around the public's reaction. It's interesting now, flipping back through those columns and being able to spot the shifts—in tone, in language, in details—how the first six or so were as cookie cutter as they come, something anyone on staff could've written. I was part of the herd, until questions surfaced that I felt only I could ask and answer. Was all that anger and sadness the public experiencing actually what true empathy was like? And was I incapable? Or was it something contrived, something conjured, something infectious and potent? If it were actually empathy, with whom did they empathize? Us members of the media, for having to cover such a story? The relatives, who hadn't spoken to Brian or Fern for years, let alone burp, change or hold Baby Cameron? Brian and Fern, for having what many speculated must have been a collective chemical imbalance? A seven-month old whose path to royalty had come to an abrupt halt?

  On the morning of June 23rd, when Tyler and Celandine Zalinski moved into the cottage across the street from Annie and me, my questions ceased, at least for a day. As I would for the weeks that followed, I watched the Zalinskis through my office window. Their Subaru Outback donned an Indiana license plate, and was the same pale shade of green as their new lawn. Some maple leaves lost in the breeze landed on the roof of the small U-Haul trailer attached to the hitch.

"Honey, I think someone's moving in across the street." The kitchen was only a room over from my office but Annie, as I thought she had for the twenty-one years we'd been married, felt it necessary to shout. "Honey?"

"I see that."

"You know who it is?"

I'd had an idea. Paul Tress, then Sports editor, had said something about Abe Wermer, then editor-in-chief, hiring some new guy from down south. "Finally got someone that knows a thing or two about basketball," Paul had said, though he often questioned Abe's judge of character. Paul estimated that the writers Abe hired for Sports lasted a month before Paul told them to get the hell out, on account that none of them were prepared for the heavy workload a small town sports writer had after the staff had been cut in half.

"You know who it is, Bruce?" Annie repeated. She tiptoed under the office's doorframe, the grey roots I loved clashing with a chestnut dye job she'd done herself six weeks earlier.

"I have an idea, yes."

"Who is it, then?"

I remember refusing to turn and address her. "I'm not sure of the details, Annie," I said, in a tone that hurt her enough that she scurried out of the office.

I watched Ray Sussoman, a sixty-something widower across the street, walk from window to window, rubbernecking for a glimpse of the new neighbors. I imagined the Thurstons, next door to us, doing the same. That's what they did when we moved in. I'd set boxes in the bedroom overlooking our property line and spot Don or Helen in the nearest window, still but featureless. They came over later with chocolate chip cookies and what I'm positive now were feigned smiles reserved for intruders.

For a moment, I wanted to return to my desk, to walk away from the window, if only to cement the differences between us. Yet, and it still isn't easy for me to say this, my time on Piney Ridge Road had shaped me into something I'd never wanted to be. I stayed put, and I stared.

Celandine Zalinski stepped out from the passenger's seat. She'd had on an orange floral dress that stretched tight along her back and hips. Her complexion was sallow. She was short, petite if not for the pregnancy. Which, when Tyler Zalinski stepped out from the driver's seat, made me wonder how she could handle such a man, not just in the bedroom, but if they ever got in an argument that escalated into the pettiest of shoving matches. His neck was thick. The sleeves of his polo shirt could've torn at the bicep. Without turning to address us onlookers, they walked to their new front door and within seconds were inside, empty-handed.

If I were right about the Thurstons, if they were indeed at a window, I don't know what they did after the big reveal. I watched Sussoman shake his head, and then walk back to his game show re-run. I smiled. I smiled because there was a U-Haul instead of some watercraft named "Whistler" or "Skidder" or "Thunderous Wake" or some other machismo name thought up by one of the hundreds of suits from Chicago or Detroit vacationing in Ludington for the summer. I smiled because the Zalinskis weren't a middle-aged couple with spoiled children who complained of the vanishing of service bars on their iPhones as they stepped onto their seasonal driveway. I smiled because they drove that Outback instead of a Range Rover.

Annie opened the office door again around 2:30p.m., holding a cookie sheet. She being so skinny then, the lavender v-neck she'd slipped into hung loose. Exercise was something she'd begun to take seriously a year earlier, including investments into weekly yoga sessions and spin classes at the community college, as well as a workout program ordered from a late night infomercial, all promising Annie the body she already had but refused to truly see.

"When do you wanna go over?"

I took a cookie. "Really? We're like the Thurstons now?"

I had no respect for the Thurstons. That much had been made clear over the years, to both Annie and the Thurstons. The few times Annie and I truly argued—nothing physical, just raised voices and words said and meant but taken back—either Don or Helen, each seeming to be graced with supernatural ears, would stop by after the dust settled and ask about our wellbeing. Which never sat well with me. Our business should be our business, and ours alone, as far as I was concerned, even on the rare occasion that things boiled over.

"It's just a nice thing to do," Annie said. "Are you almost finished with—whatever it is you're working on?"

"Not even close," I said.

Annie set the cookie sheet on the desk. "Come on," she said, stretching her fingers in a way I'd never seen, commanding Word to close my outline of Baby Cameron.

Which stood me up. I smile about the scene now but I know I said, "I didn't even fucking save that" then, and harshly. I'm not proud of it.

Annie was halfway across the street when I caught up. It was muggy outside, with mosquitoes swarming from tree to tree, from swatting hand to swatting hand. Gusts of wind blew beach sand into the road. I scanned the Zalinskis' Outback as we walked by, the Indiana Pacers decal on the back window, the ARMS ARE FOR HUGGING bumper sticker. A stack of Sports Illustrated sat on the back seat. Behind the stack rested a collapsible shovel, and beside it rested woven baskets brimming with wooden kitchen utensils.

Deputy Kramer's report had stated that there was a shovel in Brian Harris's truck. Unused, but present.

Annie, timid with their screen door, knocked on the cottage's siding. A moment later, Celandine appeared. She squinted at my tan Sperrys, her black brows creased with judgment. I stared back, at her bare feet, at the three hemp bracelets dangling from her right ankle. Her stomach was big. Water to break any day now big.

"Hello," Annie said too emphatically. "I'm Annie and this is Bruce. We live across the street."

I gave a smile that matched Annie's, a "nice to meet you" smile I could put on from time to time, for Gazette staff, for neighbors new and old.

Celandine wasn't amused. She stood still, looking like she was on the verge of saying something. In the silence, she rubbed her belly. To calm herself, I'd imagined. It took me back to when Annie was pregnant with Mark, to how she used to rub her belly in grocery store lines and while on the phone. Whenever she felt anxious, wherever she felt stressed. I thought it was such a cute tic, even more so when, years after Mark was born, I'd see Annie instinctively rub the belly that was no longer there, searching for the stress ball she'd lost.

Behind Celandine I saw Tyler walk to the door. He was groggy and rubbing his eyes, his light brown hair messy from a nap. He looked at Celandine with confusion. "Let them in, honey." He smiled at us. "We're the Zalinskis."

Celandine opened the screen door just wide enough for us to squeeze through.

"We made you guys some cookies, a welcome to the neighborhood thing we like to do," Annie said, looking at me like I had helped.

"That's really nice of you," Tyler said. He shook my hand. I still think of them as miller's hands—gritty and callused, plenty of strength to put a man of my size to his knees if he wanted. "Tyler. This is Celandine."

Celandine stepped forward. "Are they organic?"

Annie looked at me like I was supposed to know. "I don't think so," she said.

"We can't eat them," Celandine said.

Tyler looked at each of us apologetically and took the cookie sheet from Annie. "I'll eat them," he whispered, then grabbed a cookie and took a bite.

"Celandine. That's a unique name," I said.

Celandine stared at me. Squint unwrinkled now, her blue eyes looked too cold for a Michigan summer.

"It's very pretty," Annie said.

"She's named after a wildflower," Tyler said. He looked at Celandine's sharp nose, her ears and lips. A look that accepted those eyes for whatever they stood for.

Celandine kept her hand on her belly. "They're in bloom now."

"Like she is," Tyler said, then gave a goofy but proud smile expecting dads think they need to give. Ear-to-ear. "Only a matter of days."

"Do you have any children?" Celandine asked.

"A son. Mark," Annie said. "He just turned nineteen in March."

"College?" Tyler asked.

"Michigan State," I said. "Loving every second, it sounds like."

"He just left on a road trip to Colorado, with his roommates," Annie said.

Which was news to me. "He did?"

Annie nodded. "They left two days ago."

"Fun," Tyler said. "MSU, MSU—played them a couple times when I was at Butler, before we were any good," Tyler said. "Before Coach Stevenson showed up and turned everything around. Could never figure out how to stop their fast break."

I'd heard of Butler, of this Coach Stevenson, so I nodded, but I didn't have anything to add, facts, details, or an opinion. I'd always been interested in athletics, college and professional, but not enough to track stats or remember names of role players.

Unannounced, Celandine grabbed the cookie sheet out of Tyler's hands and walked out of the room, into the kitchen. It was as if she'd been thinking about what she wanted to do for some time, maybe minutes, but chose to stand in silence until something drove her to move. Water apparently, as I listened to her turn the faucet on, the cottage's old pipes revived.

"I could tell you're an athlete," I said. What an awkward thing to say. What an awkward way to break an awkward silence.

"Does Celandine play any sports?" Annie asked. Because Helen Thurston had had hip surgery weeks before on account of "pushing herself too hard" in Pilates, Annie had been looking for a new exercise buddy, but to no avail, the ladies of Piney Ridge Road claiming they had too much on their plate to commit to something like that.

Tyler shook his head. "God, no. She hates sports." He put his hands in his pockets, leaned toward us and quietly said, "I apologize if she was impolite. She's just—she's just always lived way out in the country, away from everything. A lot of new things at once can be overwhelming is all."

"Especially when you're that far along," Annie said.

"Exactly," Tyler said. "That's exactly right."

"She's fine," I said, though I did find it odd for Tyler to apologize for someone he no more than seconds earlier stared at with admiration.

"I'm sure she'll like it here," Annie said. "Lots of rural areas, lots of trees and meadows. The beach is real close, too, obviously. Plenty of outdoorsy things to do."

Tyler smiled. "I think you're right, Annie." He led us into the living room. "Please, relax and take a seat— wherever you can find one."

As we followed Tyler, a mixture of smells whirled about. The open windows let in a musty smell that mingled with the aroma of the cookies. A scent of unwashed running shoes clung to the walls of the old cottage, which was somewhat expected, as we'd watched it wither over time, unoccupied nine months of each year. I leaned against an end table flanking the green rocking chair in which Annie sat.

"So what do you guys do for work?"

"I'm home most days," Annie said, "keeping up with the house and whatnot."

"That's great. That's really great. And you, Bruce?"

"Right now I'm getting into woodcarving. Not good enough to sell them yet, but hopefully it'll pan out," I said, then wondered how unstable it made me sound to announce that first—woodcarver for eight months, columnist for nineteen years. I guess I'd decided to put my eggs in the newest basket; an issue of age, I suppose. Retirement was nearing. News was changing. Its frequency, its medium, so drastically that I'd begun to question how long a columnist with little desire to conform would be able to survive. "That's the next thing, though," I said. "I work at the West Central Gazette. I'm a columnist."

"No shit?" Tyler said. "I start there on Monday. Sports writer."

Having my assumptions confirmed put me at ease. "See, I wondered about that. I saw your license plate and I remembered we hired someone new." I thought again of the Sports Illustrated stack in the Outback. "If you don't mind me asking, why here?"

Tyler thought for a second while he chewed. "I love sports, and I love Michigan. I spent a lot of time here as a kid. Not here, specifically, just all over the state. Applied to the Free Press first and didn't get it. Cel was happy about that. She would've hated Detroit. Ludington wasn't even the second choice, just kind of happened."

Celandine walked into the room with two steaming coffee cups, her head down, focused on not sloshing or spilling. She handed the cups to Annie and me. "Herbal tea," was all she said before she sat next to Tyler on the entertainment center.

"Honey, Bruce here works at the Gazette, too."

"That's nice." Celandine folded her arms as if to say, I guess it's OK for my husband to work there, but you, I despise you for doing so. Celandine, I thought, probably didn't read or watch the news, had no respect for those working to keep the people in the know, had no idea what was going on nearby unless a sawn maple split her home when it fell.

"At least you two can carpool now," Annie said, trying to find a spot in the conversation to jump in. "Bruce just goes in on Mondays and works at home the rest of the week."

I told Annie later that she shouldn't have said that. Going to the office one day a week made me sound lazy. There were several writers doing the very same thing, though, replaced by citizen journalists who pitched stories like the First Methodist Church Bake Off or the ever-changing management of a thrift store—and get them, as well as likes and comments and shares and whatever the hell else notoriety required at the time.

"Carpooling is the least you can do if it isn't within walking or biking distance," Celandine said to Tyler. It was nice to hear some emotion instead of imagining where she hid it.

Tyler nodded agreement, then turned to me. "What do you know about that Baby Cameron story? Whole car ride that's all we heard."

No one outside of the newspaper had asked me directly about Baby Cameron, not even Annie. Nothing about the facts, nothing about the details. Nothing of my then-unformed opinion. "I'm writing a column about it right now," Despite her never asking me about my columns, despite her force-quitting my document before we ventured here, I found calmness by looking at Annie. "I've written nearly a dozen now, actually."

"No shit?" Tyler said. He liked that phrase.

"Yeah," I said. "Messy stuff."

"As fun as messy can be," Celandine said, her voice louder now. "Let's not talk about that here." She looked at Tyler, then at her belly, and then at Annie. "How's your tea?"

###

I picked Tyler up to go to the office the following Monday. Celandine was near their lone elm tree and in that same dress from Saturday, pushing clothes in a bucket of soapy water with a stick, then hanging them on a line she strung from the elm to a nearby oak after rinsing them out in a different bucket. I didn't think much of it, honestly, given that I hadn't seen a washer or dryer in the cottage the day Annie and I brought them cookies, nor had I seen a delivery truck of any sort in the days that followed. What I did find odd was the way that Celandine ignored me. She didn't look my way until Tyler came out of the cottage. He waved at me from the doorstep before he walked over and gave Celandine an "I'm off to work" kiss. Tyler then said something to her, maybe an "I'll miss you" or "Don't miss me too much", something generic I didn't think Celandine would smile at. But she did and it didn't come on suddenly and it left in no hurry.

"Morning," Tyler said, passenger door ajar. Once he sat down, he yawned and rubbed sleep from his eyes.

"Not much of a morning person?"

"Never sleep well on the couch." He waved at Celandine as we backed out.

"Sleep there often?"

Tyler yawned again. "Throughout the pregnancy, yeah. Cel isn't a great sleeper to begin with. Add in that level of discomfort and, well, you get it."

I nodded. I did get it.

"I mean, there's more to it," Tyler said. "There's more." He was quiet for a few seconds, debating the next words out of his mouth. "You saw it, you heard it: Celandine cares about the world. She cares about her health, my health, the baby's health. She cares deeply about balance." Tyler laughed. "It's infuriating sometimes, but I love that about her. I love that it so isn't how I think."

So that's how they'd come to be, I thought. Celandine gave Tyler a break from stadiums, obnoxious fans and jock straps. She'd insisted on talking about herbs or dandelions instead of final scores and draft prospects. She'd challenged him.

"Sometimes, though, I wonder if that's going to be a good thing when the baby comes, those differences. Take me, for example," Tyler said. He seemed to wake up then. "I love sports. I love cars. I love being near a city."

I wasn't sure why Tyler had decided to have this conversation with someone he'd met only days before. But, without him communicating it, I somehow understood I was the only person he could have it with, that he was desperate for someone in which to confide. Based on my lone interaction with her, I assumed Celandine would shut down as a listener, would snatch the conversation and take it elsewhere.

"But Cel, she hates sports, hates cars, hates the city." Tyler looked out the window for a while. "She even thought this place was too big. Too polluted. Too populated. And of course it isn't but—." He trailed off. "They say opposites attract, which is as true as can be with Cel and me. But to a kid, opposites are confusing, right? You know what I mean, Bruce?"

I knew. When we first started dating, what Annie had (money from Daddy, who'd been co-owner of an auto company until the recession took it under) and believed in (romance, which was what her parents were able to demonstrate over three family vacations per year, one to Miami, one to Chicago, one to Traverse City), was damn near the opposite of what I had (minimal finances, at best, thanks to a two-packs-a-day-at-the-kitchen-table mom and a nail gun dad) and believed in (work ethic, which had helped bring me out of Saginaw poverty). She had never been anything like Celandine—she would never refuse freshly baked cookies from neighbors, wash clothes by hand or make me sleep on the couch.

Degrees of our differences were presented to Mark early on. For a while he seemed to side with Annie, who talked to the walls about recent PTA meetings while she did his homework for him, who took him to the beach as a youngster and encouraged him to play soccer with boys his age, driftwood as goalposts. But as he grew older, he seemed to shift. I'd take him to the same beach some mornings, and we'd hardly talk, but just watch what was going on—the sunrisers packing up their gear, the spot-claimers setting theirs down, the joggers, those waving their metal detectors down by the shore. I wouldn't help with homework, didn't participate in any organizations—I'd been passive, wanting, expecting Mark to observe, to refine the tools it took to teach one's self, to formulate his own opinions about the world and the people within it.

Were we opposites? Did we present the idea of opposites to Mark? I don't think so. I think we what we gave Mark was the gift of multiple perspectives. It's possible that it could've been confusing to him, then. But I'd argue that a child with a wide variety of experiences will benefit later. I do still wonder sometimes, though, whether it was Annie or I who played a more crucial role in shaping Mark.

"What you're thinking about is normal," I said. "The fears that come with being a parent won't go away. You just have to take it all as it is." I turned onto Lakeshore Drive, the road Brian and Fern once lived on, the road that would take us all the way to the office, past Lakeview Cemetery and its headstone meadows. "You and Celandine are going to be just fine."

###

On Wednesday morning, I needed a rest from Baby Cameron. Though I've given it up now, woodcarving was my escape at the time. Something requiring complete concentration, something that shielded the outside noise. I'd try to carve fish, and dreamt often about the day I'd finish a salmon, or pike, or halibut. I'd become quite excited when I allowed myself to imagine a piece mine in an office, or in a living room, mounted with pride by someone who'd seen the value in my craft. It took me two years to realize my hands weren't fit for such things.

    I waited for Don Thurston's Lexus to leave his driveway, then opened the garage door to let in the breeze. While I trimmed a couple blocks of cedar with the bandsaw, I noticed Celandine in her yard. She just stood there, a dozen feet from the road, arms down, nose pointed at the sky. I wondered what she was thinking, what she was saying, if anything, if her lips were moving at all. Part of me hoped she was summoning some sort of rain-inducing abilities meant to break the streak of humidity, that soon enough she'd skip across the grass with one arm in the air, chanting incoherencies.

    She turned her attention to me once I killed the bandsaw. She didn't smile and neither did I, but I felt obligated to at least wave. Without returning the wave—again that suddenness, as if she had been thinking about how best to approach—she walked over, head down, not even bothering to look one way or the other while crossing the road.

    "Hi there," I said.

Celandine said hello, but then walked in the garage and silently looked at the ceiling, at the lone window, at the pile of wood I had next to me.

I grabbed a rasp off the bench. "Ever tried it?"

She shook her head. "Why?"

"Why? Why try it?"

She rubbed her belly and talked through a long exhale. "Why do you do it?"

"Guess I just like to." She looked away again. The Outback wasn't in the driveway. "How's Tyler?"

"He's fine."

I wondered what "Fine" meant to Celandine. Was she fine? In her mind, was she at this moment its definition? "Are you okay, Celandine? Is Tyler around today?" I asked.

She touched her belly. "He's at a baseball game in Muske-g—."

"Muskegon?"

She nodded. "Yes." She even laughed at her pronunciation. And, as brief as it was, I saw how attractive she could be, guiding her hair behind her ears, revealing a smile I couldn't help but find incredibly rewarding, something you had to work for but something so rare, something authentic you strove to witness it with regularity.

It communicated to me without her having to say so that, yes, Celandine was okay.

I relaxed. I started moving the rasp over the rough edges of the wood. "The job will take him all over the place. Just part of the deal."

Celandine struggled over her belly to grab a block of wood from the pile. Crouched, she said: "You should plant a tree for each one you carve."

"Oh yeah?"

"More and more forests are being depleted every day. You know that, right?"

There it was, her spiel. I expected a lecture that was supposed to make me feel horrible for having a hobby that involved a natural resource. "All I make is fish." I showed her how small the carvings actually were, a bit longer than my hand.

"Why fish?" Oddly, the question didn't ring of accusation, or instruction, but rather some hardened form of curiosity.

"They say it's the easiest thing to make for beginners"

She struggled to stand but waved off my assistance. "Is that true, that it's easy for beginners?"

I smiled. "Not really."

She returned the smile. "Can I see that piece, in your lap?"

It was basically a rectangle, save for one side being rounded down. I handed it to her. "It's not even close to being finished."

"Do you know when it'll be perfect?"

"Perfect? I don't think it'll ever be perfect." I watched her rotate the wood. She handed it back to me, then walked out of the garage without another word.

Because the first jury had been exposed by some citizen journalist (a Walgreens cashier by day) up from Coldwater who posted a courtroom photo to Yahoo!, a new jury for the Baby Cameron trial was being selected that Thursday. I didn't go to the selection because it wouldn't have helped me anyway—new faces wouldn't help make Baby Cameron clear.

The mistake, however, confirmed what I wanted to accomplish with this Baby Cameron column: readers needed to be challenged. A different perspective needed to be presented, where there were no sides and few questions were answered. I needed to grapple with the reader, force them to alter their posture, to reposition the weak stance they maintained. I needed to show them Brian and Fern's actions were not right, but that what is right and what is wrong is a complex construction of our minds, honed over years, over tragedy, over joy.

Lofty aim, to be sure, with a high degree of risk involved. Modern readers, as I'd been told by editorial time and again, weren't looking to be challenged. If the goal is clicks, sure, write a challenging headline. But to challenge them over the course of paragraphs? Over the course of pages? No, what modern readers were looking, according to the newspaper's editor-in-chief, Abe Wermer, was validation.

"Ask yourself then, Bruce," Abe had said the first and second times I pitched the idea of challenging our readers, "how much are you willing to pay to be told you're wrong? Tell me, how much. What's the price tag there? Because, as much as I wish it weren't the case, the roof over our heads is top of mind for me. And our roof, as you know, is on fire. The only thing that can put that fire out is subscriptions. Not Pulitzers."

He'd gone on to lecture me about community building, about the type of reader the Gazette wanted for the long haul, broken down by demographics, heaps of data split by our analytics team in dozens of ways. And I was listening. I heard him. I thought his viewpoint valid. Valid, but infuriating. Survival of the Gazette was Abe's primary goal, no matter what shape that meant the Gazette had to take. But, for me and what I brought to the table, the game Abe wanted to play was dangerous. What role can a columnist play when the directive is that all opinions must be the same? What value—true value—can a columnist add in a homogenous environment? At the expense of my dignity, not to mention the job I'd held for nearly two decades, what Abe was asking me to do, whether he realized it or not, was to tighten the leash around my neck and slowly lead myself to the slaughterhouse.

Which I wasn't yet ready to do.

So, I watched and re-watched interviews with those closest to Brian and Fern: James Harris, Lois Henslow and a childhood friend, Brock Steffes, who contacted Channel 6 after hearing of the murder, insisting he had information vital to the case. All he shared were memories of he and Brian playing tag on an elementary playground when they were nine years old. Brian was fast back then. Brock was slow. End of story.

With neither of Brian's parents living and Fern's too distraught to comment, these were the three sources from which I chose to pull. These were the three because the fact of the matter was that Brian and Fern had chosen to be outsiders. Not even their neighbors knew much about them. They claimed Brian and Fern to be good neighbors, quiet neighbors, the introverted, stay-at-home-and-binge-on-Netflix type.

To pay for their lot at Tamarac, Brian filled in at Vern Boorman's cherry farm in Scottville when work was available. But that was all. No second job. According to Lois, Fern refused to work.

A Hispanic coworker of Brian's, Thiago Morales, told me, "[Brian] always had his headphones in," when I asked about the conversations they shared. "You can ask any of us. He didn't talk much," he said. "He'd just smoke, listen to music and trim trees."

Search teams had found small quantities of marijuana taped to the inside of the mobile home's kitchen and bathroom counters, tucked in the glove compartment of Brian's S10. In their living area were stacks of vintage records but no record player. The likes of Los Bravos, Ian Whitcomb, The Kingsmen, obscure 60s artists that to my knowledge had never been touted as the next best thing, let alone by Brian and Fern's generation.

That night, as I squeezed a tension ball, I convinced myself that this column would be my take, that it should be my take. No one else's. Everyone else had had their say and, as instructed, I'd echoed it as far and wide as I could. But not this time.

I convinced myself that there were no more meaningful facts of the Baby Cameron case to include, that they'd all been used up, that things like Baby Cameron's murder happen across the country, and often. Happen to couples who love. Happen to couples who love, then hate, then love each other again in a matter of hours. But infanticide doesn't just occur because of fluctuating emotions. It can't. There has to be influence from something else. Someone else—relatives, parents, grandparents, friends, whomever hints at the incapability of successfully raising a child, an insecurity planted deep in the brain. But to introverted outsiders like Brian and Fern, what does successfully raising a child mean? More importantly, who or what told them they weren't capable?

And what of the death? Something could surely be said about how Fern killed her son. Could I say it was better that she drowned Baby Cameron instead of having Brian grab his arms and fling him against a car door? Could I say it was better Brian put Baby Cameron in a ditch next to one of the most driven roads in Mason County so he could be found quickly instead of placing him in the woods where coyotes would tear him to shreds?

"Nice and slow," I heard Tyler say outside. My window was partially open.

"I want to have it here."

From the office window I watched Tyler guide Celandine down their front steps.

"Honey, we've been over this. We can't have it here." Tyler opened the passenger door of the Outback for her. "They told us that months ago, remember?"

Celandine stood under the porch light. "I don't want their drugs," she said. I held onto this thought for some time afterward, wondering if one day I'd be able to spot rows of cannabis planted behind the cottage.

"Just get in the car, Cel."

For a moment I think Celandine saw me watching from the window, noticed the two pried blinds. I know she did. I know she saw me and I know that's why she got in the car. Which brought back memories, of Sussoman and the Thurstons watching from their porches as I hustled Annie to the car, a pressure I not once sought heaping on my shoulders by the second.

The next afternoon, I watched Tyler jog into his house with an empty canvas bag I assumed he'd pack with organic food Celandine requested from her hospital bed. When Tyler came back out, he looked tired as hell. Shoulders slumped, clothes wrinkled from sleeping in a bedside chair, hair jutting out like a bluejay's.

I said through my open office window: "Slow down, big guy."

Confused, Tyler searched for where the voice came from. I think it could've been this kind of naïveté that drew me to Tyler. Celandine knew exactly where to look.

"It's Bruce," I said. "How is everything?"

Tyler located my window. "It's good. Everyone's healthy. Just grabbing a few things."

"Boy or girl?"

"Girl," he called out. As Tyler got into the car, I spotted a folded sky blue blanket tucked under his arm and it made me think of Deputy Kramer's report, then wonder if Celandine had planned on a boy, had declined to know its sex but had held onto a hunch.

Annie walked into the office with our dog, Jess, a two-year old mutt Mark brought home as a present for Annie before he went off to college, citing that his mom needed something to take care of once he was gone. "Who are you yelling at?" she asked, getting Jess's leash ready for their routine walk around Hamlin Lake.

"Tyler. They had a girl."

After Mark, Annie had always wanted a girl. "That's great," Annie said, and for a moment I think I could see envy reach across her cheeks. "Maybe it'll soften Celandine up a bit."

###

That Saturday was beautiful. Little humidity, not a cloud in the sky and somewhere near seventy-five degrees, Annie, along with most of the neighborhood, was outside. Jess was tied up under the shade of our maples by the road, panting when not barking at dogs and their walkers passing by. The Thurstons sat in patio chairs near their mailbox. Sussoman wrestled with some weeds in his one flower bed of petunias and chrysanthemums. Annie worked on her rosebush below the office window, trimming heavy branches that had made it lean east. I watched her work the sheers, admired the wrinkles on her triceps that she wished would go away. The rest of the neighbors, I assumed, were by the lakeshore, on beach towels, or on the sandbar splashing water at each other. I even heard a powerboat, probably "Whistler," skidding across its own wake and thought it a peaceful thing.

All day I'd been sitting in my office wondering if ever I could put myself in the shoes of Brian and Fern Harris, if I could find it in me to kill my own son, either as the pudgy baby that he was or as the thin blonde-bearded young man he'd become. There was no way. Just contemplating it nauseated me. But that didn't mean that it was completely immoral for Brian and Fern. Did it?

What I was stuck on: I took a philosophy class in college that gave students a hypothetical situation. You were in a burning art museum and you could either choose to save the Mona Lisa from one room, or save an abandoned baby from another. You could only carry one. You had to ask yourself, "What would be better for the world? Most of my classmates sided with saving the baby, their argument being that it's a life that has yet to be lived, full of potential good. But I, as well as a guy named Duncan, chose the Mona Lisa.

Duncan proceeded to argue that the money made by selling the Mona Lisa to the highest bidder, it being the world's most valuable painting, could provide food, water, and shelter to thousands of people in need. "It was the humanitarian thing to do," Duncan had said.

I didn't disagree. But that wasn't my argument. I chose the Mona Lisa because Adolf Hitler had once been an infant. And Timothy McVeigh. And Osama bin Laden. I chose the

Mona Lisa because one should not ignore the opposite of the argued potential good. I chose the Mona Lisa because the fact that a baby is stranded doesn't mean that one day they won't perform acts of evil, however catastrophic.

On her evaluation of our arguments' strength, the professor deemed myself and Duncan the victors. When class was dismissed, there was a young woman—I don't recall her name—who came up to me with wet eyes, her finger pointed at my chest. "Baby killer," she said. And she said it one more time before walking off.

I figured I'd add that anecdote somewhere in the column, maybe even start with that girl pointing her finger at me. But the more I thought about the Mona Lisa, the more I kept seeing Mark as a baby. His eyes, I swear, were the size of bottle caps, his hair silky, his feet only a third of my hand. Not once did I think this child of mine could hurt anyone, destroy anything, not with those feet, not with those hands or tongue. He was only capable of building and helping and being kind and decent.

I went back to the death of Baby Cameron, the actual act of murder. Neither parent had appeared to act out of hate. A violent act fueled by hate would've resulted in blood or bruising. Several stabs of a knife. Shoving him through a wood chipper. That wasn't what happened. Not that a seven-month old could put up much of a fight, but there were no bruises. No scrapes, no fingernail marks.

"Must've just held 'em down gently," the medical examiner, Irvine Lang had told me, when I believed facts would serve as the spine of the column. He shaped his large, gloved hands into the position he imagined Fern using. "Minimal pressure on either the head or lower back. They were careful not to use force."

Is there morality in that? And, if the murder was not committed out of hate, what was it then? Fear? And what were the origins of that fear? Maybe they saw some kind of emotional blemish in their son the night he was born, something that planted within them a feeling that the kid would discard every opportunity to come his way, that he'd evolve into the next Manson or Bundy. Maybe they saw him one day reaching for his steak knife at the dining room table and running the blade across his arm. Maybe at six months old he'd banged his head on the floor repeatedly instead of trying to crawl. Could violence inflicted upon the self be a sign? Not that early, right? Still, left to the imagination were scenes of Brian and Fern passing a bowl, eating microwaved dinners and watching their son, sharing a stare that said it was time.

My cell phone rang. It was Mark. I'd called him earlier that day. The thought of murdering him had made me long to hear his voice. He was out of breath when he answered.

"Something wrong, Mark?"

"No, no, I'm fine. Just had to run up a hill to get service." He yelled to one of his roommates to be quiet. "You called earlier. What's up?"

"Been busy. Your mom, too." Mark yelled for someone to grab him a beer, which wasn't something he'd do if Annie were on the line. He was nineteen at the time, almost twenty—I knew underage drinking would happen and had accepted that fact, had even convinced myself that it was better for him to binge at nineteen than at twenty-nine. Get it out of his system. Still: "You guys being careful?"

"Of course, Dad. Listen, can I call you back? About to get back on the road, and I'm losing you."

It had been Tyler's turn to drive into the office, but I insisted I give the new father a break. I picked him up and, as gloomy as that Monday was, as gloomy as it could've been for him, with his parental leave nixed, to this day I still haven't seen him so giddy. He told me they'd named her Ivory. He told me again and again how beautiful she was, how indescribable of a feeling it was to hold her, to have his finger wrapped by her hand. I was happy for him. I said so. Told him to cherish such things.

"Zalinski, you get that piece about the Bobcats done?" Paul Tress asked as we walked into the office. Paul—broad shoulders, toucan nose, big gut buoyed by suspenders—was an intimidating man, but even more so when growling questions like this.

"Mr. Tress, I apologize, but no, no I don't have it done," Tyler said. Paul settled his weight on his heels and crossed his arms. "My baby girl was born this weekend."

"I know. I know." Paul sighed. Seemed to bat scenarios around in his mind about how to handle everything. "Just get the story to me by this afternoon, if you can," Paul eventually said. He nodded at me. "Newhouse, good to see ya."

"You believe that guy?" Tyler asked me after Paul was out of earshot.

I chuckled. "He likes you."

Abe Wermer appeared soon after Paul walked away and, right on cue, said: "Bruce, where are you at with the new Baby Cameron column?" Thin and pointy, I'd always likened Abe to a swizzle stick. "We're going on two weeks now." I knew that all too well.

"Making some headway," I said. Over the weekend, I had, but not as much as Abe would've liked. He'd preached time and again that in today's world quantity was far more important than quality.

"Well, we all hope so. Tick tock," Abe said. Then he slithered back to his office and shut the door.

"Can you believe that guy?" I said. Tyler found that very funny.

I sat at a vacant desk near Tyler's. My working primarily from home for the past months had been Abe's suggestion, a way to cut office costs. But in doing so, I discovered through reflection that I'd always found it difficult to get any work done at the office. When I started at the Gazette the problem had been how noisy the place was, the incoherent chatter, the constant punching of keys. But then it had become increasingly difficult because of that noise fading away, the emptiness that came with a slashed staff. All would be quiet except for three or four employees lightly typing on laptops or conducting interviews over office phones.

On his way to the coffee pot, Tyler stopped at the desk I was at. "I think me and Cel will bring her by tomorrow, after I get back," he said. "If that's okay with you."

I told him that Annie and I would love to see her.

He smiled as he walked off. "My family, will be coming over," he said and continued to practice while walking. "My family."

But they never did.

It was approximately 11:15p.m on Tuesday night when the Zalinskis' porch light came on. I walked to the window and watched a shadow, Tyler's—too big of a body to be Celandine—walk along the driver's side of the car. His right arm was chickenwinged, edges of that same sky blue blanket swaying. I could barely make anything else out before he arrived at the car. Only a bit of his face: his eyes, his mouth. From this distance, from this angle, for that split second that he looked down at the blanket, all I could register was that they looked incredibly sad. I watched him open and close the driver's side door, start the car and back out of the driveway.

I called the Zalinskis' cottage. No answer. No interior lights flipped on, not even when I walked over and knocked on the door. No one rustled around inside. No baby cried. Tyler had to have her—that's what he was carrying. But why? Where was he going? Diapers? Formula? The curves of Pere Marquette Road?

Walking back to the house, I thought of the Baby Cameron photos kept from the public, one in particular given to me upon request showing Baby Cameron's bare head frozen to a piece of ice. Once broken by Strauss's vehicle, the ice angled towards the bottom of the ditch. There were splotches of skin where Baby Cameron's head had ripped away. His eyelashes had turned into tiny icicles.

I didn't want to wake Annie. There was no need, let alone time, so within minutes I was backing the Corolla out of the garage.

There were a few other cars on the road, some heading north, some south and all traveling much slower than me. When the Outback came into sight, I slowed down. I don't know why. I could've driven alongside Tyler and pointed to the shoulder of the road but I didn't, and I don't know why. I could've made him stop but I didn't, and I don't know why. Doing so would've saved so much time. Instead of confronting him then and there, I hung back until the Outback turned right onto M-116, then followed.

Had Tyler ever been north of Ludington? Or west? Did he even know where he was going? Where was Celandine sending him? Or maybe this was Tyler ditching her plan. Maybe this was Tyler improvising. But Celandine killed that baby. I knew she had. Tyler couldn't have done it.

He'd been too happy, too damn happy. I imagined a birthmark on the neck she despised, a shortened finger that couldn't be corrected, an imperfection not even a rasp could smooth.

I noticed breaks in thin clouds. The tops of trees outlining the State Park. The moon, stars here and there. Other than the taillights of the truck, some Ford I kept between myself and Tyler, it was the only light. Once the truck turned right into a large parking lot by public restrooms and picnic tables, I slowed down again. I don't know why I was so adamant on keeping distance between us, but I did, and it allowed me to see the lake between gaps in tree branches. It was calm and it made me question my participation in this, if this was the columnist in me, the father, the friend, or if distinction between one another was even possible.

A couple miles later Tyler turned left into the parking lot of Big Point Sable, a non-working lighthouse turned tourist attraction. I knew, I just knew he was going to leave his daughter here, where she could be found easily by some cubicle dweller on a morning jog, by some kid whose errantly-thrown football dinged the dead girl's forehead. Police cars. News vans. Months of speculation. Repeat.

Tyler drove to the front of the empty parking lot, parked, and shut the car off. The interior light came on in the Outback. His head turned toward the road. I drove a couple hundred yards further, away from Tyler, so as not to be spotted. I parked far away, shut my headlights off, and continued watching Tyler. He opened the Outback door and stepped out, his arm chickenwinged once more. I watched him walk toward the lighthouse, and then shifted back into drive and slowly made my way toward the front of the parking lot, headlights still off.

Now out of my car, I looked through the dark windows of Outback. There was nothing out of the ordinary in the back seat—an empty car seat, the same stack of Sports Illustrated, the same woven baskets now empty, granola bar wrappers, and sunglass cases. There was no baby bottle, no blankets, no box of diapers, no rattles. But there no longer was the collapsible shovel. Because the shovel was in his free hand. It had to be. He wasn't just going to set her on the ground; Tyler was going to bury his daughter.

I don't know what I planned on doing but, because I didn't immediately dial 911, I must've maintained some level of doubt. Not enough for me to stop telling myself that I couldn't let that happen, whatever it was that was happening. I couldn't turn the other way and run. And does that make me fine? Does that make me better than fine? Does that make me decent?

    I walked toward the lighthouse. The wind was colder there than at home and I heard waves rolling to shore, breaking sporadically. Dune grass shivered atop mounds of sand on each side of the boardwalk leading to the lighthouse. A freighter's beacon of light shone way off in Lake Michigan, which made me think of shipwrecks, of Tyler and his dead daughter and what happened, what Celandine saw wrong. But then I heard a wail, a grown man's wail. I waited until I heard another one, then tried to locate where it came from. Walking toward the sound, I pictured Celandine filling the kitchen sink and holding the baby by her feet until she stopped wiggling. Plugging the nose, covering her mouth with bare hands. I walked further, wondering if I'd somehow played a part in this.

    A gust of wind.

    Our conversation in the garage. She'd wanted her baby to be perfect. But it wasn't. It couldn't be.

    Waves breaking.

    I looked to my left and saw a silhouette sitting atop the sand.

    Wind. Waves.

I walked closer. My voice cracked when I said, "Tyler?"

The silhouette shifted. "Bruce?"

I looked at Tyler's lap, where Ivory lay, blades of dune grass inches from her ears. Her face was expressive. Her legs moved.

"Bruce, are you okay?"

"It's just that you, uh, you guys didn't come over today." Tyler adjusted his posture. The baby girl's head moved. Her eyelashes moved. Everything moved. "And when I saw you leave I—I." I put my hands on my hips and looked out at the lake. I felt my stomach turning on itself. "I'm sorry," I said, wiping my mouth.

"I'm sorry I didn't let you know. I totally spaced. Little miss Ivory here has been pretty restless." Tyler ran his fingers through what little hair she had. "Paul didn't seem too happy when I called in but he said he understood. Now that Cel's finally asleep I wanted to give her some peace and quiet, you know?" Tyler caught me staring at Ivory's feet, at the pink socks covering ten wiggling toes.

I flattened some dune grass next to Tyler and sat down. Sand trickled past the tongues of my shoes and it made me calmer, sinking. At that moment I tried to remember where the Mona Lisa was. France, I was sure. The

Louvre. But I didn't care, really. Let the painting burn. "So Celandine's doing okay then?"

"She's just exhausted. I mean, she was exhausted before labor. Tack that on, and then adjusting to a new home life, I'm sure it'll take a little time."

A decent person taking their turn in this conversation would have said that Celandine was going to be fine, that she'd be a great mother, maybe that she already was. But I couldn't bring myself to. Each detail disproving what I'd expected, what I'd tricked myself into believing made me feel like a harpooned sturgeon brought on deck to be cut open.

"I'm sorry," I said.

"For what, Bruce?"

I wanted to confess my troubles with Baby Cameron to Tyler. I wanted to tell him how confused I was that Ivory was fine, that I would've been relieved if his baby girl were dead because that would've made me feel certain about at least one thing. "When I was walking up, I thought I heard you crying."

"Crying? Really? No, no, I was humming," Tyler said, straightening his legs slowly, Ivory descending with them. "I guess we were a little loud, weren't we, little girl?"

That was a cry, I knew it was a cry. He couldn't have been humming, a hum couldn't be so loud. "What were you humming?"

"It's cheesy," he said. "You'll laugh. 'Row, Row, Row Your Boat'. She loves that song. Well, I think she does anyway." Tyler offered Ivory to me. "You want to give it a shot?"

I forced a smile. "You go ahead."

Tyler hummed, and it was loud, until that freighter tugged its horn. Ivory cried at the deep sound. Tyler lifted her and swayed her back and forth until her crying subsided.

We talked about the Gazette for a while, about Tyler's next big assignment (Ludington High School football offseason workouts) until Ivory fell asleep, then walked to the parking lot. I'd been so far in my head that I'd left the Corolla running.

"I'll be right behind you," Tyler said, setting Ivory into her car seat carefully.

"Look." I had to say it again. "I'm really sorry. I'm not usually like this." No, the usual Bruce packed himself tightly in his office and stared out a window to assume, to speculate, to tell himself lies about things he thought he understood.

"Bruce," Tyler said. "Stop apologizing. We're friends, right? I'm sure it looked suspicious as hell, me loading up a newborn late at night and driving off." Tyler patted my back and had I not had my feet shoulder width apart, I may have toppled over. "It's great here though, isn't it?"

"Yeah."

Tyler followed until I stopped at a Wesco and bought a cup of coffee. Before I went in the house, I rearranged tools and swept sawdust in the garage because that's all I felt like doing, that's all I felt I was capable of. Annie woke up to me rounding out a fish's sides so I told her, "I couldn't sleep," over and over until she, still concerned, went into the house. I called Mark's cell phone and told his voicemail I loved him, wherever he was, whomever he decided to become. And before I went to bed, I wrote by hand not about Baby Cameron, but about the Zalinskis, about neighbors, about how the Harrises had conditioned me to think of mine as murderers. I wrote that I was wrong and circled it at least twenty times.

RASP

a *Strays Like Us* story by Garrett Francis

ABOUT THE AUTHOR

Garrett Francis is the author of the novel *And in the Dark They Are Born* and the short story collection *Strays Like Us*. He grew up on a small farm in Michigan and earned his B.A. in Creative Writing from Grand Valley State University.

In 2012, Garrett co-founded *Squalorly*, a digital literary journal of the Midwest and served as its nonfiction editor until 2014.

In 2016, founded Orson's Publishing in 2016, a micro press and served as the press's sole editor (and designer, and publicist, among other roles) until its closure in 2020, publishing four book-length works by new and emerging authors.

He also founded *Orson's Review* in 2017, a digital literary journal that served as a companion to its parent press, publishing fiction, creative nonfiction, poetry and photography. He served as the sole editor of *Orson's Review* as well, and is proud to have helped bring the work of over 70 international contributors to life.

Today, Garrett lives in the Pacific Northwest with his family. Short works of his have been published in literary journals like *Midwestern Gothic*, *Barely South Review*, *Whiskeypaper* and *Monkeybicycle*.

###

Visit authorgarrettfrancis.com to learn more about Garrett and his work.

Copyright © Garrett Francis, 2024.

All rights reserved. No parts of this book may be copied, distributed, or published in any form without permission from the publisher. For permissions contact: authorgarrettfrancis@gmail.com

This is a work of fiction in which all events and characters in this book are completely imaginary. Any resemblance to actual people is entirely coincidental.

ISBN: 978-0-9914463-7-7

Published by 5626 Press

Milton Keynes UK
Ingram Content Group UK Ltd.
UKHW042125211024
450028UK00010B/108

9 780991 446377